DISCARD

WELCOME TO THE CONSTRUCTION SITE

Dump Truck

Samantha Bell

Published in the United States of America
by Cherry Lake Publishing
Ann Arbor, Michigan
www.cherrylakepublishing.com

Content Adviser: Louis Teel, Professor of Heavy Equipment Operating, Central Arizona College
Reading Adviser: Cecilia Minden, PhD, Literacy expert and children's author

Photo Credits: ©Kustov / Shutterstock, cover, 2; ©Eng. Bilal Izaddin / Shutterstock, 4; ©Eduard Dvorchuk / Shutterstock, 6; ©icealien / Shutterstock, 8; ©TS Photographer / Shutterstock, 10; ©Andrey N Bannov / Shutterstock, 12; ©jennyt / Shutterstock, 14; ©Dmitry Kalinovsky / Shutterstock, 16; ©Mikbiz / Shutterstock, 18; ©sanek70974 / Shutterstock, 20

Copyright ©2019 by Cherry Lake Publishing
All rights reserved. No part of this book may be reproduced or utilized in any form or by any means without written permission from the publisher.

Library of Congress Cataloging-in-Publication Data
Names: Bell, Samantha, author.
Title: Dump truck / by Samantha Bell.
Description: Ann Arbor : Cherry Lake Publishing, [2016] | Series: Welcome to the construction site | Audience: Grades K to 3. | Includes bibliographical references and index.
Identifiers: LCCN 2018003279| ISBN 9781534129184 (hardcover) | ISBN 9781534132382 (pbk.) | ISBN 9781534130883 (pdf) | ISBN 9781534134089 (hosted ebook)
Subjects: LCSH: Dump trucks--Juvenile literature.
Classification: LCC TL230.15 .B44 2016 | DDC 629.225--dc23
LC record available at https://lccn.loc.gov/2018003279

Cherry Lake Publishing would like to acknowledge the work of The Partnership for 21st Century Learning. Please visit *www.p21.org* for more information.

Printed in the United States of America
Corporate Graphics

Table of Contents

5	Carrying Materials
13	Heavy Loads
15	Ready for Anything
21	Helping Others
22	Find Out More
22	Glossary
23	Home and School Connection
24	Index
24	About the Author

Carrying Materials

Dump trucks have **containers** on the back.

What do you carry?

They carry **materials** to the **construction site**. They carry materials away from it.

Some carry dirt or sand. Some carry **gravel** or rocks.

Some carry construction **debris**.
Some trucks can carry up to 100 tons!

Heavy Loads

A dump truck has a lift. It pushes up one end of the container. The materials slide out.

They can go on soft, muddy ground. They can go on hard, rough ground.

How do more tires help a dump truck?

Some trucks have 4 wheels. Some have 6 or 8 wheels. Some have 10 or 12 wheels!

Helping Others

Dump trucks keep things moving!

Find Out More

Book

Graham, Ian. *Dump Trucks and Other Big Machines*. Buffalo, NY: Firefly Books, 2016.

Website

The Great Picture Book of Construction Equipment
www.kenkenkikki.jp/pbe/carry/carry_002.html
Learn more about dump trucks at this site.

Glossary

construction (kuhn-STRUHK-shuhn) the job of building
containers (kuhn-TAY-nerz) objects such as boxes, jars, or barrels that are used to hold something
debris (duh-BREE) the pieces that are left after something has been broken or destroyed
gravel (GRAV-uhl) small pieces of rock used on paths and roads
materials (muh-TEER-ee-uhlz) things you need for a project or activity
site (SITE) the place where something was, is, or will be built

Home and School Connection

Use this list of words from the book to help your child become a better reader. Word games and writing activities can help beginning readers reinforce literacy skills.

a	from	moving	soft
away	go	muddy	some
back	gravel	of	the
can	ground	on	they
carry	hard	one	things
construction	has	or	tires
container	have	out	to
containers	heavy	pushes	tons
debris	it	rocks	truck
dirt	keep	rough	trucks
dump	large	sand	up
eight	lift	site	wheels
end	loads	six	
four	materials	slide	

Index

construction site, 7
containers, 5, 13

debris, 11
dirt, 9
dump trucks, 5
    how much they can carry, 11, 15
    how they work, 13
    what they carry, 7, 9, 11

wheels, 19
where they can go, 17

gravel, 9

lift, 13

materials, 7, 13
mud, 17

rocks, 9
rough ground, 17

sand, 9
soft ground, 17

tires, 15

wheels, 19

About the Author

Samantha Bell has written and illustrated over 60 books for children. She lives in South Carolina with her family and pets.

DISCARD

E BELL FLT
Bell, Samantha,
Dump truck /

01/19